W. Elfe Tayler

The End not yet: A Reply

SALZWASSER
VERLAG

W. Elfe Tayler

The End not yet: A Reply

Reprint of the original, first published in 1859.

1st Edition 2022 | ISBN: 978-3-37513-250-7

Verlag (Publisher): Salzwasser Verlag GmbH, Zeilweg 44, 60439 Frankfurt, Deutschland
Vertretungsberechtigt (Authorized to represent): E. Roepke, Zeilweg 44, 60439 Frankfurt, Deutschland
Druck (Print): Books on Demand GmbH, In de Tarpen 42, 22848 Norderstedt, Deutschland

THE END NOT YET:

A REPLY

TO

DR. CUMMING'S NEW WORK,

"THE GREAT TRIBULATION,

OR,

THE THINGS COMING ON THE EARTH."

BY

W. ELFE TAYLER,

Author of " Papery, its Character and Crimes ;" " Hippolytus and the Christian Church of the Third Century ;" " The Last Days," &c., &c.

"AND YE SHALL HEAR OF WARS, AND RUMOURS OF WARS ; SEE THAT YE BE NOT TROUBLED : FOR ALL THESE THINGS MUST COME TO PASS, BUT THE END IS NOT YET."

—MATT. xxiv. 6.

𝔅𝔯𝔦𝔰𝔱𝔬𝔩:
PUBLISHED BY W. MACK, 52, WINE STREET.

𝔏𝔬𝔫𝔡𝔬𝔫:
WERTHEIM AND MACINTOSH, PATERNOSTER ROW.

1859.

CONTENTS.

CHAPTER I.

Dr. Cumming's Theory of the "Great Tribulation."

BEFORE entering upon the task of disproving the extravagant and absurd theory which Dr. CUMMING has brought before the public, as to the approaching end of the world, or present dispensation, it will be proper to state clearly what that theory is. We shall do this in his own words, for two reasons. First, because it is always more satisfactory to the reader, and more just to the writer to do this; and, secondly, because Dr. CUMMING has said so little about prophecy, throughout his whole work, that it will be easy, in the compass of a few pages, to place before the reader nearly the whole of it. Here is a book of *four hundred and seventy-nine pages*; yet, will it be believed? there are scarcely a *dozen* pages consisting of direct prophetical exposition. There are grand prophetical *titles* of lectures—and striking prophetical *texts* of Scripture for mottos to lectures, and running titles, on the top of every page,—but very little in the Lectures themselves on the subjects thus paraded before the eye. A more disappointing book, in this sense, we never remember to have perused.

B

The first chapter of the book is full of promise. It is on "The Glorious Deliverance." The text of Scripture selected as the motto is,—" And at that time shall Michael stand up, the great prince which standeth for the children of thy people; and there shall be a time of trouble, such as never was since there was a nation *even* to that same time : and at that time thy people shall be delivered, every one *that shall be* found written in the book" (Dan. xii. 1).

"I accept," thus commences the author, "the generally received opinion of commentators, that Michael, the prince that standeth for the ancient people of God, is not a created angel, but our Lord and Saviour Jesus Christ. The prophecy seems to imply that having long been seated on his throne as Mediator, interceding in behalf of his own, that man's extremity will become his opportunity; and that he will stand up towards the close of this present Christian economy, amid miracles, and stupendous phenomena, and great and startling issues in behalf of his cast-off, but not finally cast-out people,. the remnants of the house of Judah and of Israel. It is plain from the language, 'thy people,' addressed to Daniel, an inspired prophet, and yet an enthusiastic and patriotic Jew, that the interposition of Christ on this occasion will be primarily in behalf of that remarkable race still preserved, often assailed, but never crushed ; like their own burning bush, always blazing, and not consumed ; and that the time will come when they, so long cast out, shall at length be grafted in, and restored to their own land ; for a Deliverer, as quoted by the Apostle in the Epistle to the Romans, shall come out of Sion, and shall turn away unworldliness from all the children of Jacob. 'Thy people,' therefore are primarily the Jews."

Then follows, after a long digression, about the dispersion of the Jews, and the abduction of the Jewish boy Mortara, and the residence of the Prince of Wales in Rome, and so forth :—

"At this period of trouble Christ interposes; having no sympathy with him that assumes to represent him, and stands up amidst stupendous miracles of mercy and of unobliterated love, in behalf of a people persecuted, a by-word, a scoff and a hissing among all nations ; restores them to their land ; replaces them in their ancient and illustrious capital. . . . .

"But when this takes place, there will be a time of great trouble. 'At that time there will be a time of such trouble as has not been on the earth since there was a nation;' and which is stated in the New Testament to be a time of such trouble that there never will be any trouble equal to it. We have that time of trouble delineated in St. Matthew, where, after some portraits of the judgments upon Jerusalem, he gives a reference, clear and unmistakeable, to the close of this present economy. The great time of trouble began in 1848 : in other words, it synchronises with the pouring out of the seventh vial ; at which the first shock of the great European earthquake occurred : its succeeding shocks still steadily occur, year after year. Review at your leisure the events that have transpired since that time. Why we are no sooner out of one trouble—I mean the world—than we are plunged into another. In 1849, Europe, Asia, America, were desolated by an overwhelming pestilence ; in 1850, Rome, anticipating its ruin, made its last spasmodic grasp or clutch at the sceptre of England, if perchance it might retain a last footing before it goes down into the depths of ruin. In 1851, we had a bright glimpse, by way of symbol, earnest, or type of millennial peace. Then, after that we had the first hint of the complications in the East ; then, from 1854, a war which has sent streams of bitterness into many a happy English home, and left cold shadows upon many a once-bounding English heart. The dead that sleep in the distant Crimea will not soon be forgotten ; and I trust the memories of the brave that fell there will never come before us without thanks and gratitude for those that so heroically fought, and many of them so hopefully and piously fell. No sooner had the Russian war been closed, than the great Indian storm burst upon Asia ; an Empire was in peril ; and again how many homes have lost their brightest lights in consequence of that cruel, atrocious, and murderous outburst of a deceived, infatuated, and misguided native population ! No sooner had that been lulled, by God's blessing on the heroism of our troops, and the sagacious diplomacy of those who had to rule the storm, than, like a thunder-cloud, we saw all Europe mustering to battle ; and upon the beautiful plains of Italy half a million of men met in deadly conflict, and thousands are numbered with the dead. I stated before, what many thought, was impossible, that Russia's destiny was the East. We read in some of the papers, on what authority I don't know, but I infer from the quarter it must be right, that Russia now combines with France; and two such powerful autocrats would seem to be a match for the whole world."

" I believe that our own land, whatever be the combination that girdles it—even as if it should girdle it with fire—is destined to emerge comparatively unscathed from the conflict; and old England's sun will not set till it mingles with the splendour of that sun that shall have no cloud and no western declension. We separated from the great Apostacy at the Reformation, and God has blessed us ever since, and God will bless us still; and I believe, with all our faults—and we dare not deny them, and we would not conceal them—there is in the depth of our nation a piety, a living religion, unprecedented in its history, and with which no other nation in its spiritual condition can for one moment be compared."

After mentioning the occurrence for the first time of a Hebrew word in Rev. xix., as a proof that the restoration of the Jews is referred to in that striking prophecy, we read :—

" Now at this very time, mark you, when the judgments come upon the great apostacy, where you hear the voice of the Jew clear and unmistakeable in the great anthem peal, you will find at the close of the chapter a picture of the tribulation which Daniel makes synchronous with these two grand events. ' I saw heaven opened, and behold a white horse ; and he that sat upon him was called Faithful and True, and in righteousness he doth judge and make war. And he was clothed with a vesture dipped in blood :' the language of awful conflict. ' And out of his mouth goeth a sharp sword, that with it he should smite the nations ; and he shall rule them with a rod of iron; and he treadeth the wine-press of the fierceness and wrath of Almighty God.' And then mark what takes place : ' And I saw the beast'—the wild beast, the symbol of the great western apostacy—'and the kings of the earth, and their armies, gathered together to make war against him that sat on the horse, and against his army.' And what was the issue ? ' And the beast was taken, and with him the false prophet '—the exponent of his voice, the priesthood—'that wrought miracles before him. These both were cast alive into a lake of fire burning with brimstone.' The word *brimstone* is derived from the German, and means simply *burning stone.* 'And the remnant were slain with the sword of him that sat upon the horse, which sword proceeded out of his mouth.' Now, that chapter seems evidently to synchronise with the verse on which I have now been commenting in Daniel xii. Well, then, 'All thy people shall be delivered;' that is, in the midst of the judgments which I have delineated, or rather, which I have read, God's ancient people, if this refers to the Jews, as I think it does, as well as the first clause, 'shall be delivered.' And the apostle, speaking of this very event, makes the striking remark, 'If the casting away of the Jews has been the reconciling of the world, what shall the receiving of them be but life from the dead?' All Israel, he says, shall be saved; and God shall turn away ungodliness from Jacob. The branches that were broken off shall be grafted in, and God's goodness as well as severity shall be exhibited in their case."

The author then goes back 1800 years, and gives us, by way of variety a lecture on the destruction of Jerusalem by the Romans, under the title of "*The Doomed City.*" Then comes Lecture 3rd, "*The Great Convulsion, or Shaking of Nations.*" Surely, we said, here at last we have some real prophetical exposition, about the future of Europe. But we were mistaken. The whole lecture is upon the existing condition of the missionary cause—the present state of Europe and the world generally. Not half a dozen sentences are occupied with prophetical exigesis. Still worse in this particular is Lecture 4th, on "*Things Coming on the Earth.*" This being the very subject of the book— which bears the title of "THE GREAT TRIBULATION: OR, THE THINGS COMING ON THE EARTH"—it was natural to suppose, that here at last we should certainly find the views of Dr. CUMMING fully set forth, supported by the statements of Holy Writ. But no such thing: it is a disquisition on the declension of religion in the churches of Christ generally, mixed up with a description of the famine of

Ireland, the cholera of 1854, and the earthquake that took place in 1857 in Italy. To illustrate this last, two long letters from the *Times'* correspondent are inserted verbatim, reaching through nearly six closely-printed pages !

Then follow lectures on "*Evening Clouds,*" "*The Last Witness*"—that is, the preaching of the Gospel throughout the world ; and many other poetical and romantic-sounding titles, such as "*Evening Light,*" "*The Standing Miracle,*" "*Nearing Deliverance,*" "*The Day and the Hour,*" "*The Glory-filled Earth,*" &c. At last we get (at page 240) a lecture on "1867," and here we find something more befitting a work professedly on Prophecy. The motto of the lecture is Dan. xii. 11, 12,—"And from the time that the daily sacrifice shall be taken away, and the abomination that maketh desolate set up, there shall be a thousand two hundred and ninety days. Blessed is he that waiteth, and cometh to the thousand three hundred and five-and-thirty days."

The following is the substance of the author's remarks on these very important dates of Daniel :—

"What I shall endeavour to show now is this, that whatever theories of the fulfilment of these dates are held, whether they fix the commencement at this period, or at that period, or at some other period, nearly all concur in one remarkable conclusion, namely, that 1867 is to be the great crisis, the testing crisis in the events of history, in the fulfilment of prophecy, and in the experience of mankind. What I wish to show is, that the best, the wisest, and the most thoughtful of writers on the subject of prophecy, however much they may differ in certain details—and they do differ—nearly all coincide in this, that 1867 is to be a great crisis ; and that if all that some expect to occur at that period do not occur, we are at least on the eve of events, as Lord Carlisle has expressed it in his work upon Daniel, the most stupendous, if not ushering in the very close of this present Christian economy, we must carefully weigh the quotations, that thus we may be able to judge whether the data on which these writers have come to their conclusions be correct or not.

"ELLIOT and MEDE have shown that the 2300 years, which Daniel gives as one of the great chronological epochs, terminate about the year 1821 or 1822; that is, dating them from the march of Xerxes and the meridian splendour of the Persian empire. But a very learned and able clergyman of the Church of England, who has written a work called 'The Terminal Synchronism of Daniel's Two Periods' differs from Mr. ELLIOT. He thinks that the 2300 years, one of Daniel's great epochs, after which, as I showed you, the Eastern Apostacy, or the waters of the river Euphrates that should overflow Europe, that is, the power of Mahomet, should begin to subside, began at the autumnal equinox of 433 B.C.; and if the 2300 years began at the autumnal equinox of 433 B.C., then that great period would terminate in the autumnal equinox of 1867. ELLIOT's opinion was that the 2300 years measure out the taking away of the daily sacrifice, and the exhaustion of that great eastern eclipse which was to overshadow the light and the sunshine of heaven in the eastern world, and that they end in 1821; at which time Mahometanism as a power in Europe was shaken to its centre, and began to cross the Bosphorus, and to fall back upon its ancient channels in Asia, and to cease to be a dominant triumphant, and advancing fanaticism. But this writer thinks that the proper date is 433 B.C.; and if so, then they would terminate in 1867, when, according to him, Mahometanism will be utterly expunged, and the cross will shine where the crescent now waves in triumph. But more than this; this writer thinks also that the expression 'time, times, and half a time,' which all commentators admit to be 360 years, twice 360 years, and 180 years, making altogether 1260 years, called in the Apocalypse, 42 prophetic months, which is the same thing, called also 1260 prophetic days—start from A.D., 607. Mr. ELLIOT, and NEWTON, and MEDE, think that the 1260 years, descriptive of the great Western Apostacy, began at the year 532, at which era Justinian constituted the Bishop of Rome to have supreme civil, ecclesiastical, and spiritual jurisdiction; they consider that at that period the Apostacy was invested with supreme civil and ecclesiastical power, and therefore with its permanent form as a politico-sacerdotal system. But this writer differs from them; he says that the 1260 years do not begin at 532 after Christ, but that they begin at the year 607, when the Emperor Phocas constituted

Pope Boniface III. the universal head of the universal church, and the supreme and chief bishop, priest, and prelate of Christendom. If you take this latter opinion, then you add the 1260 years to the year 607, and it brings you down to the same period at which his 2300 years terminate, namely, 1867 ; and according, therefore, to this theory, not only will Mahometanism totally cease at that period, but the Papacy also, with its pope and its cardinals, and its whole ecclesiastical despotism, will sink like a millstone into the depths of the ocean ; and the world east and west, emancipated from the incubus that has crushed and darkened it, shall reflect the beams of an unsetting sun, and form a portion of that great empire which constitutes the kingdom of our God and of His Christ. I must say I prefer Elliot's ; but what I wish to impress is, the remarkable fact, that both interpretations land us in 1867, as a great dominant era, characterized by stupendous events, and involving mighty changes in the present constitution of things. The theory adopted by the interpreters I prefer, is that the 1260 years which were to mete out the dominant power of the Great Western Apostacy began in A.D. 532, when Justinian, in his 'Pandects,' gave the supreme authority to the Bishop of Rome. If you add 1260 years to 532 it brings you down to 1792. Accordingly, at the exhaustion of the 1260 years, in 1792, the Papacy, according to the description in the word of God, was to come under the judgment of Heaven, and gradually to be exhausted. Read 'Alison's History,' or any other authentic history, and you will find that the great outburst of the French Revolution in 1792 commenced so overwhelming an onslaught on the Papal power, with all its dependencies, that from that day to this Romanism has been a dying system, exhausted of its chiefest vitality, and struggling for a foothold in any land to which it can have access ; so much so, that I have repeated again and again the conviction, that I have no more fear of Popery gaining the upper hand, than I have of Mahometanism or Hindooism gaining supremacy. . . .

" Assuming that 532 began the 1260 years, what is next to take place, Daniel tells us in this passage, to which I specially ask attention. as confirmatory of the theory I am trying to uphold, that first of all there shall be time, times, and half a time, or 1260 years, and then there shall be 1290 years. In other words, Daniel says that 1260 years shall be augmented by 30 years more ; at the end of which 30 years there shall be some great event, which we have to ascertain. Now if we add to 1792, when the 1260 years terminated, an additional 30 years, it brings us down to 1822.

But 1822 is the terminating period of the 2300 years also, according to Elliot's interpretation. Well, did anything take place in 1822 that could justify that period as a terminating epoch? We find that Turkey, in the language of Lamartine, began to die for want of Turks; the whole force of that great system of propagandism then began its rapid exhaustion; and from that day to this even our efforts to keep back Russia have not kept up Turkey; it is at this moment in the pangs of dissolution. I stated four or five years ago that it would be so; and however justified we were, and we were justified in trying to prevent Russia from disturbing the balance of the power of Europe; yet, as I then said, our efforts to preserve Turkey would be vain. Russia has still a signboard near Petersburgh, on which is written 'The way to Constantinople;' and in the lapse of years Constantinople will be hers, and Russia will yet play a part in the history of the world probably unprecedented for a thousand years.

But Daniel says 'Blessed is he that waiteth, and cometh to the thousand three hundred and five and thirty days.' Here is still an additional period. He adds 75 years to the 1260, or 45 years to the 1290. He mentions three periods, you observe, all beginning, we here assume, at 532; first 1260, ending in 1792; then 1290, ending in 1822; and then 1335, ending in 1867; so that, according to this theory, Daniel's period, when he shall be blessed or happy that waiteth, and cometh to the close of the 1335 years, that period assumed by ELLIOT to be the millenial rest, would begin in the year 1867, and last for a thousand years of uninterrupted felicity; and blessedness, and peace. But what I wish to impress is that, according to both theories, 1867 again evolves as the year of stupendous changes. And it is very remarkable too, what will confirm this, and what I shall quote passages to prove that FINES CLINTON, the ablest chronologist of the age, has shown, and I think with irresistible force, that our era at present, namely 1859, is not the correct and real era in the chronology of the world. His idea is that Christ came about the year of the world 4138; and that in the course of a few years more we shall have arrived at the close of the sixth thousand, and at the commencement of the seventh thousand year of the world. What it is interesting to show in connection with this is the universal belief among Jews and Gentiles, Rabbinists, Talmudists, and Fathers, that the seventh thousand year of the world is to correspond to the seventh day of the week; six days the working week, and the seventh day the Sabbath-day rest; 6000 years for the working world week, and the 7000th year to be what the apostle describes as the rest, or the σαββατισμὸς, that remaineth for the people of God."

After citing Mr. CUNNINGHAM, of Lainshaw, the late Rev. EDWARD BICKERSTETH, and Mr. SCOTT, in favour of the year 1867 as a great prophetical era, Dr. CUMMING proceeds :—

"I have given these extracts from competent authorities, all coming to one conclusion—that the seventh thousand year of the world is to be its millenial rest; and I have shewn you that, if the chronology of Mr. FINES CLINTON be correct,—and *I am satisfied it is correct,*—we are at this very moment within eight years of the close of the sixth thousand year, and therefore, if our dates be right, *within eight years of the commencement of* what all these writers hope is *the everlasting rest, the dawn of heaven, the* millenial blessedness of the people of God."

There can be no mistake as to the real opinions of Dr. CUMMING. According to a Chronology which he is "satisfied is correct," *the year* 1867 *will be the commencement of the millenium,* and, consequently—as he is a firm believer in the pre-millenial advent—the period *of the coming of the Son of man* "with power and great glory."

CHAPTER II.

The Great Period of Twelve Hundred and Sixty Years.

THE capital error of Dr. CUMMING—so far we have any insight into the meaning of Divine Prophecy—consists in this, that he regards the *twelve hundred and sixty years*, or *time, times, and half a time*, as already past. He expressly says that they closed in the year 1792, the era of the first French Revolution. As the result of this serious mistake —as we regard it—by adding together the two supplemental periods of *thirty* and *forty-five* years, the author is enabled, with some show of probability, to represent the year 1867 as the time of "the coming of the Son of man." If the reader will favour us with his attention, it will be easy to show, that the great era denoted by the close of the "time, times, and half a time" is *not yet arrived*, and that not only the testimony of prophecy, but also the events of history, unmistakeably prove, that we are now living under the period spoken of by Daniel and John, in various places of their prophecies, as the twelve hundred and sixty days.

Such of our readers as are familiar with that wondrous book — the Apocalypse of John — cannot fail to have observed, that the ONE great subject which appears on almost every page, is—the joint reign for a definite period, of two symbolical wild beasts—and their fearful overthrow at the time appointed. Other important topics are introduced, it is true: and occasionally these occupy some considerable space. But this is principally on account of their connection with the one great subject of the Apocalyptic page; and in order to illustrate more fully the character of the two leading actors in this wondrous drama.

According to some of the ablest modern expositors of prophecy, these two symbols denote *Civil and Ecclesiastical Despotism.* The *Ten-horned* Wild-beast (Rev. xiii. 1—8) is the "world power," as AUBERLEN terms it, as represented by the kingdoms which arose on the ruins of the Roman Empire. The *Two-horned* Wild-beast (Rev. xiii. 11—17), which "exercises all the power of the first beast before him"—is the Ecclesiastical power, not of Rome merely, but of the Greek Church also.

Now, the period during which these two Antichristian powers bear rule is variously stated, as "a time, times, and half a time"—"Forty-two months"—and "twelve hundred and sixty days." But these various expressions amount precisely to the same period—on the commonly received year-day principle—of twelve hundred and sixty years. What we are particularly desirous, however, of impressing on the reader is, the *character* of this period. For, throughout the Prophecies both of Daniel and of John, this is uni-. formly represented as the hour of darkness and of woe—the period of oppression and of crime. The Ten-horned Beast—the modern kingdoms of Europe—enjoys a period of uninterrupted success and prosperity for 1260 years, "blaspheming God and His tabernacle, and them that dwell in heaven"—"leading into captivity, or killing with the sword," all that oppose his will, and "shedding the blood of saints and of prophets," whilst God stands by, waiting for the set time for deliverance to come. "And power was given unto him to make war *(margin)* forty and two months." (Rev. xiii, 5).

During precisely the same period, the Second Beast—the spiritual ally of the first—exercises similar dominion in spirituals to what the secular beast does in temporals. There is thus presented before our eyes a complete *imperium in imperio.* The Ecclesiastical power corrupts Christianity into a system of despotic rule ; and, whilst in the plenitude of its power, the Western branch subjugates even the Civil power to its sway. Hence we find, at a later period, Rome represented as riding upon the ten-horned beast, (Rev. xvii). This Western branch, too, of the corrupt universal Church, joins the first beast in its ruthless crusade against God's people, and is said to be "drunk with the blood of the saints, and with the blood of the martyrs of Jesus." This harlot of Rev. xvii is identical with the little horn of Daniel, which "makes war with the saints" (vii. 21).

In order to illustrate more fully the character and conduct of these two great enemies of God and His Christ, the church, during this disastrous period, is set forth under a two-fold emblem. In the 12th chapter we find her exhibited as "a woman clothed with the sun, the moon under her feet, and a crown of twelve stars on her head"—preserved, by the providence of God, in the wilderness during the *twelve hundred and sixty years.* In the other—for the purpose of exhibiting them in their character of protesters against the tyrrannous and blood-thirsty rule of the Civil and Ecclesiastical powers—the people of God are represented as "two witnesses;" the one denoting probably the line of individuals who have boldly protested against the usurpations and crimes of the *Civil despotisms* under which Europe has so long groaned. The other, the noble army of martyrs who have sealed with their blood their testimony against "Babylon the Great." * These two witnesses of God are said to "prophesy in sackcloth" during the whole period of *twelve hundred and sixty days*, to signify the gloomy and distressing character of the times during which they live. At the close of this period, the ten-horned beast—the Civil power—"makes war against them, and kills them," and not satisfied with their destruction, vents his implacable rage upon their unburied remains (Rev. xi., 7, 9).

It us thus plain, we think, beyond all contradiction, that the period of twelve hundred and sixty years is the era, on the one hand, of the reign of the two Anti-christian monsters of the Apocalypse—Civil and Ecclesiastical Absolutism : and on the other, of the depressed and perse-cuted state of the church of God—considered under the two-fold aspect of the woman hidden in the wilderness, and of the two witnesses prophesying in sackcloth. It re-presents the exaltation and triumph of the great enemies of God and man, and the consequent distress and humiliation of the chosen remnant of Jesus Christ. It is, to use Isaac Taylor's expression, the dark MILLENIUM of all

---

* Another interpretation deserving of notice, is that which makes the two witnesses the true church of God in the East and West—during the time of Antichrist.

that is evil and terrible in man, in which it would seem a license had been granted to infernal spirits to invade earth with the practices of hell !

It is impossible to conceive a more striking contrast to this melancholy state of things than that which succeeds, at the expiration of the *twelve hundred and sixty days*. Then, the Seventh Trumpet utters its welcome blast, and "great voices are heard in heaven, saying, the kingdoms of this world are become the kingdoms of our Lord and of His Christ, and He shall reign for ever and ever" (Rev. xi. 15). Then, "the judgment sits, and the dominion of the beast is taken away, to consume and to destroy it unto the end" (Dan. vii. 26). Then, the church quits her asylum, and stands forth as the sun-clothed woman described in the 12th chapter of the Apocalypse. Then, the saints of God, hitherto under the power of the scarlet-clad harlot—Babylon the Great—are set free from her bloody grasp. Then, the two witnesses—no longer doomed to prophesy in sackcloth—are exalted to heaven, the emblem of safety and honour—dignity and power. Lastly, the "great voices in heaven" proclaim that "the wrath of God is come, and the time of the dead [martyrs], that they should be judged" [avenged] (Rev. xi. 18). And, as the result, Seven Angels are commanded—"Go your ways and pour out the vials of the wrath of God upon the earth" (xvi. 1).

Having thus briefly pointed out the very decided and marked contrast between these two eras—we are desirous that the reader should ask himself the question—under which of these two distinct periods we are now living ? To which of these two eras is the present state of things in

Europe to be assigned? Is the great period of the twelve hundred and sixty days, during which the Apocalyptic wild-beasts bear sway, still running on? or has that dark and dreary period passed away, and given place to a morning of light and gladness which shall ere long brighten into one eternal day of glory?

If we ask Dr. CUMMING, and some other writers of that school, they will tell us the latter is the true answer to this deeply interesting inquiry. The twelve hundred and sixty days of trial and suffering have long since gone by. They expired at the breaking out of the First French Revolution in 1792 (1789 would be more correct). Then it was, that the Seventh Trumpet uttered its welcome sound. Then it was, that the angels having "the seven last plagues," in which "is filled up the wrath of God," issued from the Temple. Then it was, that the five first of these vials were poured in quick succession upon France, and the other Continental Kingdoms; and we ourselves are witnessing, in our own day, the effects of the effusion of the fifth, in the slow but certain decay of the power of the Turkish Empire.

Now, there are two methods by which it would be easy for the reader to satisfy himself that the author of the "Great Tribulation" is here in error; the one, is to look at the present state of the Continent of Europe, and contrast that with the promised peace, prosperity, and glory of the church of God under the Seventh Trumpet! The other, to enter upon a course of prophetical argumentation, and thus show, from the position of the Seventh Trumpet in the Chart of Prophecy, that its blast cannot possibly be already past.

In the first place, then, is it not notorious that, in the present day, the two great Curses of Christendom—Civil and Ecclesiastical Despotism—still hold absolute sway, throughout nearly the whole Continent? Europe, from the Atlantic to the Vistula, is filled with the groans of the oppressed, and the cries of the persecuted. Unquestionably, France, Spain, Austria, and Italy, exhibit *not* such a state of things, in a political or a religious point of view, as to indicate that Absolutism and Popery had received their death-wound seventy years ago; but, rather, the continued existence of those accursed systems, in almost all their wonted activity. It is true that, during the last few months, the Papacy has experienced a severe blow, in the loss, for the present at least, of the best part of her temporal dominions—but it is extremely doubtful whether this will prove a permanent loss. If it should, the Ecclesiastical Supremacy of the Pope will not be affected by it—and it is this that constitutes (together with the Greek Church) the two-horned beast of the Apocalypse. At any rate, leaving out the events of these last few months, it is beyond dispute that for a long time the whole Continent of Europe, except two or three of the smaller States, has been prostrate beneath a despotism, both Civil and Ecclesiastical, so rigid as to tempt one to believe that the dial of time had gone backward, and that we were once more about to return to the gloom and misery of the dark ages.

It must be confessed that this is a remarkable state of things, if, indeed, the reign of the two Apocalyptic wild-beasts had come to an end seventy years ago. A marvellous contrast does this present to what we should naturally expect if the twelve hundred and sixty years had so long

C

since come to a termination. Still more strange, if, as Dr. CUMMING and others assert, the joyful blast of the Seventh Trumpet sounded in 1792.

Surely, no impartial inquirer into the fulfilment of Divine Prophecy, as he thinks upon the forlorn and hapless condition which Europe has presented to the eye of the Christian philanthropist for the last half-century, can believe that before the commencement of that period, the Church of God emerged from the wilderness—the two witnesses no longer prophesied in sackcloth, but occupied the place of power in heaven,—the power to change times and laws was taken out of the hands of the Papacy,—and the persecutors of the saints of God ceased to rule.

Secondly, the same thing may be proved by referring to the page of Divine Prophecy. When did the second woe terminate ? What event in the history of the past has ever fulfilled the death and ascension of the two witnesses ? When did the *third woe*, mentioned in Rev. xi. 14, as quickly following the ascension of the witnesses, take place ? Where can we find the fulfilment of the plagues of the seven vials, in which is filled up the wrath of God ? Yet all these things and many other events plainly happen before the period of the Millennial Blessedness which Dr. CUMMING tells us is so near—viz., in 1867.

It cannot, then, be doubted, we think, that Dr. CUMMING has made a grievous mistake in thus publishing to the world—re-echoed as it is in the pages of the *Times* —the announcement that the great prophetical period of the "time, times, and half a time," has already ended; that it terminated in 1792; and has since been followed by the sounding of the Seventh Trumpet, and the effusion of the

Seven Vials which are "to destroy them that destroy the earth." He has evidently failed to read aright "the Signs of the Times." He has confounded together two periods as different from each other as light and darkness. He has described as a period of glad deliverance, a time in which as every one can see, priestly bigotry and ecclesiastical despotism have well-nigh crushed Continental Protestantism; and he has assigned to the glorious period of the Seventh Trumpet a state of things in which is dominant a tyranny more hateful than that of the Cæsars.

There can be little doubt, that the mistake just referred to, into which not only Dr. CUMMING but other writers on Prophecy have fallen, is mainly to be attributed to the impression produced on most minds by the events of the first French Revolution. It cannot be denied that many of the results of that unparalleled outbreak of the popular will bore considerable analogy to those which according to the "sure word of prophecy" are to succeed the expiration of the twelve hundred and sixty days. Christian men then living on the earth were thus naturally led to indulge the expectation that a new and brighter era was dawning upon this benighted world. Those conversant with the history of that terrific period, will remember that as one of the results, free constitutions were obtained by some of the European States, the interests of civil freedom were promoted also in many other ways; and the religious benefits which it conferred were neither few nor trifling. It is remarkable that about the same period a great Revival of Evangelical Religion took place in England; and the modern missionary spirit dates from the same era. Various societies were set on foot for the conversion of heathen nations, and the general diffusion of the Scriptures. Whilst openings for the preaching of the Gospel occurred in many countries of Europe immersed in Papal darkness and superstition.

What wonder, amid such events as these, if men did think that a new and glorious era of light and happiness had at length dawned upon the world!—That men who witnessed these blessed results of that terrific moral earthquake felt impressed with the conviction that the dark millennium of priestcraft and absolutism was passing away, and the long-expected era of light and liberty, truth and righteousness, setting in. There is no reason, however, that we, in the middle of the nineteenth century, should commit ourselves to the same blunder. We, that have lived to see our fondest hopes frustrated ; that have witnessed these glorious influences spend themselves ; and have seen how a re-action, in every part almost of Christendom, has taken place. It would be the height of folly for us to suppose that the French Revolution of 1791 was the death-knell of Civil and Ecclesiastical Despotism, and the harbinger of freedom and salvation to suffering humanity. Beholding, as we do, the results of that tremendous convulsion, from the vantage-ground of futurity, we can readily discover that the Revolution wanted depth of principle and stability of purpose. It possessed the brilliance of the meteor that shoots momentarily athwart the sky, but it wanted the steadiness and duration of that light " which shineth more and more until the perfect day."

CHAPTER III.

The Seven Vials, yet future.

IT must be admitted, then, that the great period of twelve
hundred and sixty days is still running on—the two Anti-
christian systems, which occupy so prominent a place in
the Apocalypse, are still ascendant in Europe, and as a
consequence the church of God is still in the wilderness,
and the two witnesses prophesy in sackcloth, and shut
heaven that it rain not.

Another necessary consequence which follows from the
foregoing remarks is the fact of the Seven Vials being still
future. Dr. CUMMING and some other writers on Prophecy
speak of these "plagues" as having been already poured
out. We have already witnessed, he tells us, the effusion
of the Sixth Vial, and the present decay of the Ottoman
Empire is the result of that Vial being poured on "the
Great Euphrates," causing "the waters to dry up." But,
if the "twelve hundred and sixty days" be as yet un-
expired, it is obvious that the Vials must be still future.
To any one who peruses with care the Apocalyptic description of these "seven last plagues," it will be evident, that
they are retributive judgments upon the two beasts of the

Apocalypse, for the terrible arrear of crimes which have for twelve centuries past been accumulating. The *first* Vial is poured "upon the men which had the mark of the beast, and them which worshipped his image;" the *fifth* is poured on "the seat of the beast, and his kingdom is filled with darkness, and they gnaw their tongues for pain." And as to the *seventh*, its chief result is, that "Great Babylon comes in remembrance before God to give unto her the cup of the wine of the fierceness of His wrath.—Besides this, it is expressly said, that these Vials are "the seven LAST plagues;" and that in them "is FILLED UP the wrath of God." So that they completely finish the work of vengeance, and utterly destroy those guilty systems from the face of the earth. To suppose, then, that such terrible and final judgments as these can be inflicted during the period of the "twelve hundred and sixty days," while those guilty systems are running their course of prosperity and triumph, is utterly irreconcileable with reason and common sense.

Yet, further, as matter of fact, no fulfilment of these Seven Vials of Divine wrath can be pointed out in the history of past. The events to which Dr. CUMMING, and some other writers on prophecy, direct our attention as constituting the accomplishment of these marvellous predictions, are, as we conceive, of the most unsatisfactory kind.

The FIRST VIAL—"a noisome and grievous sore, upon the men which had the mark of the beast, &c."—is said to have been poured out at the first French Revolution, and it denotes, we are told, the *prevalence of infidelity and irreligion* in France and the adjoining countries. But, so far as we understand the meaning of the symbolical language of Prophecy, this interpretation is altogether a mistake. If there be any meaning in language, *a noisome and grievous sore* denotes some direct and obvious source of torment and misery. It denotes that, in like manner as persons suffering under the bodily disease mentioned, are constantly harassed and plagued with those eruptions, so would the miserable objects of this First Vial groan and writhe under the torment of this divinely-inflicted " plague." How did the infidelity and irreligion, so rife in France during the first Revolution, occasion incessant pain and suffering to the people of that land? So far from this, there can be little doubt, that in throwing off the shackles of religion, they were just following the bent of their own inclinations. We cannot, then, for a moment, accept this as an accomplishment of the effusion of the First Vial; and as nothing better, so far as we are aware, has hitherto been suggested, we abide by the opinion already expressed, that this fearful infliction of Divine wrath is yet future.

The SECOND VIAL, under which the sea becomes " as the blood of a dead man, and every living soul therein dies," is interpreted of the *destruction of the naval forces of the various kingdoms of the Papacy*, by the British Admirals. But these victories fall far short, we think, of the fearful character of this plague. The naval achievements of Hood, and Howe, and Nelson, brilliant as they were, come very short of the ideas suggested by the expression just quoted. Besides events very similar to these have frequently occurred in the history of modern Europe—and it is in the highest degree improbable that such occurrences should constitute one of the " seven *last* plagues, in which *is filled up* the wrath of God." We may further add, that such an interpretation appears altogether to overlook that meaning of the symbol employed, which it everywhere bears in the Apocalypse. The sea denotes " peoples, and multitudes, and nations, and tongues" (Rev. xvii. 15).

The THIRD VIAL is considered by this school of expositors to refer to the victories of the French Republican armies on the Danube, Rhine, and other rivers. It is true, these military achievements were attended with tremendous slaughter, but the question we have to ask is simply this,— in what particulars did these conflicts differ from other engagements, so far as to be styled one of the "seven last plagues in which is filled up the wrath of God?" Unquestionably, the recent battles of Magenta and Solferino were far more sanguinary and fatal.

As regards the FOURTH and FIFTH VIALS, the supposed accomplishments of these predictions are, if possible, still more unsatisfactory than the above. Nothing approaching to the "sun scorching men with great heat," and the wretched victims "blaspheming God, who hath power over these plagues," has ever yet occurred. Nor has the kingdom of the beast ever yet been "smitten with darkness," so that "they gnawed their tongues for pain." This expression beyond all question intimates such a state of horror and despair as the abettors of tyranny and oppression have never yet experienced.

The SIXTH VIAL (which is represented, by Dr. CUMMING, throughout the "Great Tribulation," as poured out,) can be shewn, still more clearly than either of the preceding, to be yet unfulfilled, because there is a general agreement among all writers on Prophecy, that this prediction relates to the

Ottoman Power. The Sixth *Trumpet* appears clearly to denote the overthrow of the Eastern Empire by the Turks, in 1453; and, similarly the Sixth *Vial*, as is generally agreed, denotes the extinction of the power of this same nation, under the symbol of the drying up of the waters of the Euphrates. A century and a half ago, MEDE, the father of modern Prophetical exposition, expressed this opinion:— "It is in my opinion," says he, "the Ottoman Empire, which will then be the only barrier to these new enemies from the East." The same opinion is expressed by nearly all Expositors since his time.

We ask, then, has this prophecy of the drying up of the waters of the Euphrates received its fulfilment? Or, at least, is it now in course of fulfilment? We read in Dr. CUMMING's work that the Sixth Vial was poured out in 1822; "then," says he, "Turkey began to die for want of Turks; the whole force of that great system of propogandism then began its rapid exhaustion." At the time of the Russian war, too, we remember Dr. CUMMING, in common with a number of other writers spoke in the most confident terms of the past effusion of this Vial on Turkey, and predicted as the consequence the speedy conquest of that power by the Russian arms. On the testimony of witnesses of unquestionable authority, however, it may be shown that the facts of the case do not agree with these *ex-parte* statements. It is said that, during the Russian war, ABDUL MEDJID was able to oppose the army of the Czar with no less than 200,000 soldiers, in addition to which there was a body of reserve comprising 150,000 men. This did not look like a nation whose population had been dried up by the Vial of Divine wrath, twenty or thirty years before.

A speech of LORD PALMERSTON, delivered in the House of Commons during the same period, is worthy of notice, as bearing upon this question :—"I do not at all admit," says his Lordship, "that the Turkish Empire is in the state of decay represented by the honourable gentleman (Mr. Cobden). The honourable gentleman is wholly misinformed as to the state of Turkey for the last thirty years. I assert it without fear of contradiction, that Turkey, so far from having gone back within the last thirty years, *has made greater progress, in every possible way, than perhaps was ever made by any other country during the same period.* Compare the condition of Turkey now with what it was in the reign of Sultan Mahmoud. . . . . I venture to say that Turkey has made immense progress during the period I have mentioned. So far from talking of Turkey as a dead body, an expiring body, or something which cannot be kept alive, I am satisfied that if you will only keep out of it those who want to go into it, there are countries in Europe that are in much more danger of sudden dissolution from internal causes than Turkey." Now, we put it to the candid reader, whether it be within the bounds of possibility, that an enlightened Statesman at the head of the Government of Great Britain could have expressed himself in such language as this about a country whose waters had been dried up by the effusion of this last plague, thirty years before? Beyond all doubt, then, we believe the Sixth Vial is yet future—and when, in the Divine counsels, the time for its effusion has arrived, it will be accomplished in such a terrible judgment upon that land of the Eastern Antichrist as shall leave no room for question or dispute relative to the actual fact. "The waters of the" figurative "Euphrates" will be completely "dried up," and thus "the way be prepared for the Kings of the East."

The remarks of Dr. CUMMING relative to the *Seventh Vial,* which he regards as, in all probability, poured out in 1848—and his idea that its being "poured into the air" is fulfilled in the morbific miasma prevalent during the last ten years—shows its force in the potato, the vine disease, and in altered normal condition of health and disease, are really hardly deserving of notice. How any intelligent christian man can read that awful prophecy contained in Rev. xvi. 17—21, and see its fulfilment in such petty troubles as these, we are at a loss to understand. As this Vial forms the subject of a subsequent chapter, it will be unnecessary to dwell upon it here.

If the views advocated in this chapter, as to the Vials being still *future,* be correct, it is obvious we are furnished with another powerful argument against the theory of Dr. CUMMING, relative to the rapid approach, and extreme proximity of the end of the present dispensation. The infliction of a succession of judgments such as these must, in the very nature of things occupy some years, yet they have not yet commenced. Still more, there is nothing to indicate that their effusion is near at hand. Nay, prophecies which must receive their accomplishment before the era of the effusion of these Seven Vials, are not yet fulfilled—the death of the witnesses, their ascension into heaven,—the earthquake in which "seven thousand names of men [margin] are slain" (xi. 13) and "a third part of the city falls,"—the restoration of the Jews, &c. &c. Taking all these considerations into account, then, we think,

the sober student of Prophecy will be disposed to think
many years must yet intervene before the word of our
blessed Lord are applicable—"when these things begin to
come to pass, then look up and lift up your heads, for your
redemption draweth nigh" (Luke xxi. 28).

CHAPTER IV.

The Year One Thousand Eight Hundred and Sixty Six.

WE have no sympathy with those who discourage the study of *unfulfilled* Prophecy. This is, as we think, to defeat the very object for which Prophecy was given to the church—"to shew unto us things which must shortly come to pass." Prophecy is in fact "a light shining in a dark place" whereunto we shall "do well to *take heed*," instead of leaving it, as so many Christian men of the present day, would have us do, until it has been fulfilled. If a torch is given to a traveller to carry with him in journeying along a dark and dangerous road, he does not consider its principal use to be by holding it behind him, to shew the dangers he has passed, but he thrusts it before him into the darkness to ascertain those which loom ahead. So, we maintain that Prophecy is not given to the church that after its fulfilment we may compare the prediction with the event, and thus derive fresh evidence of the truth of religion. This is undoubtedly *one* end. But a far higher object, we believe, is contemplated by the blessed God, in conferring this vast boon upon the church. It is given to cheer, to encourage, and support the people of God in their passage through the wilderness of this world—by showing that "the triumphing of the wicked is but short," and that a period is rapidly approaching for the downfall of the enemies of God, when the church shall at length come forth from her hiding-place —and "Gentiles shall come to her light, and kings to the brightness of her rising."

We do not find that Daniel waited thus for the accomplishment of the prophecy respecting the captivity of his people, the Jews. On the contrary, he tells us, that he studied the import of this prediction whilst it was yet *unfulfilled Prophecy*, and as the result we are informed that "he understood by books the number of the years whereof the word of the Lord came to Jeremiah the prophet," &c. (Dan. ix. 2.) Why, too, we would ask, should such special blessings be pronounced on the students of the Apocalypse by the Spirit of God, even when that book was first given to the church if *unfulfilled* prophecy be, as many would tell us, forbidden ground? "Blessed is he that readeth, and they that hear the words of this prophecy, and keep those things which are written therein, for the time is at hand." Such is the opening passage to this sublime and mysterious book (Rev. i., 3). And the close is very similar :—"Blessed is he that keepeth the sayings of the prophecy of this book" (Rev. xxii. 7). How is it possible to reconcile these repeated statements in the book itself, if it be true that unfulfilled prophecy should be carefully avoided by Christian men?

In the previous pages we have attempted to show that the opinion of Dr. CUMMING, as to the "coming of the Son of man" and close of the world happening in the course of the next eight or ten years, is altogether devoid of any Scriptural foundation. It must not be supposed, however, that there is no truth in his statements about the year 1867. On the contrary, we are fully prepared to admit, that the year specially referred to by him, will, very probably, constitute a great crisis in the history of Europe and of the world. It seems to be the turning point in the career of the two Apocalyptic monsters,—*Civil and Ecclesiastical Despotism.* It is also the commencement of a bright period in the history of the Church. In short, there is abundant reason to believe that the great period of "twelve hundred and sixty years"—the era of oppression and violence—persecution and woe to God's people—will about then come to a close, and judgments, in quick succession, begin to fall on the two great enemies of Christ, .the *world-power*, represented by the 'ten-horned beast,' and the *Apostate church*, in alliance with her—the 'two-horned beast' of Chapter 13th.

It would be difficult, within the whole range of human inquiry, to name a more important and deeply interesting question than that which forms the subject of the present chapter :—viz., When does the great period of "twelve hundred and sixty days" come to a close? To the Christian—to the philanthropist—to the mere worldly politician,—what can equal in importance the inquiry,— How near are we to that great *crisis* of Military and Ecclesiastical Absolutism and Tyranny predicted in the Apocalypse? Let us attempt, then, with all seriousness and soberness to place before the reader the solid evidence on which rests our firm belief—a belief not lightly taken up, but one held for the last twenty years—that we are now on the

eve of this great and critical era, and that in, or about, the
year 1866, Europe will be the theatre of a Universal Revolution, which will permanently change the whole aspect of
things, and be the precursor of a period of light and
liberty, holiness and happiness to this sin-filled world.

We shall first premise that, beyond all question the two
beasts of the Apocalypse exercise a joint reign or dominion
during a period which is variously stated as " a time,
times, and half a time"—" forty and two months," and " a
thousand two hundred and three score days"—and, as a
necessary consequence, the people of God are the victims of
their joint cruelty and violence during the same period.
The following are the only places where the period in
question is mentioned. " And he shall speak *great* words
against the most High, and shall wear out the saints of the
most High, and think to change times and laws ; and they
shall be given into his hand, until a time, and times, and
the dividing of time."—(Dan. vii. 25). " And I heard the
man clothed in linen, which *was* upon the waters of the
river, when he held up his right hand and his left hand
unto heaven, and sware by him that liveth for ever, that
it shall be for a time, times, and an half ; and when he
shall have accomplished to scatter the power of the holy
people, all these *things* shall be finished."—(Dan. xii. 7).
" But the court which is without the temple leave out, and
measure it not ; for it is given unto the Gentiles ; and the
holy city shall they tread under foot forty *and* two months.
And I will give *power* unto my two witnesses, and they
shall prophesy a thousand two hundred *and* threescore
days, clothed in sackcloth."—(Rev. xi. 2—3). " And the
woman fled into the wilderness, where she hath a place

prepared of God, that they should feed her there a thousand two hundred *and* threescore days. And to the woman were given two wings of a great eagle, that she might fly into the wilderness, into her place ; where she is nourished for a time, and times, and half a time, from the face of the serpent" (Rev. xii. 6 & 14). "And there was given unto him a mouth speaking great things, and blasphemies : and power was given unto him to make war [margin] forty *and* two months" (Rev. xiii. 5). It will be observed that, in these passages, it is not the *duration* or existence of these systems of oppression and tyranny that is referred to, as constituting the period of twelve hundred and sixty days, but their *ascendancy* and *prevalence* in the earth, and the persecuted condition of the true church, as the natural result.

Several of the passages just quoted will afford us very little help in attempting to fix the *terminus a quo* of this great Prophetical period. Perhaps the most useful for our purpose, because the most definite and precise, will be the *first*,—from Daniel's remarkable prophecy of the four Universal Monarchies under the image of so many wild beasts arising out of the sea. Out of the head of the last of these—which by general consent is interpreted of the Roman Empire—the prophet observes a little horn spring up. This unquestionably denotes the Papacy or Western Church, afterwards symbolized, in conjunction with the Eastern Church, by John, as a *two-horned* beast, in the 13th of the Revelation. Of this little horn the prophet says, " He shall speak great words against the most High, and shall wear out the saints of the most High, and think to change times and laws, and they SHALL BE GIVEN INTO

D

HIS HAND until a time, and times, and the dividing of time" (Dan. vii. 25).

Now, on the assumption that this little horn, according to the most able commentators, denotes the Papal See, let us inquire whether the records of Ecclesiastical History furnish us with anything like a fulfilment of this delivery of the "times and laws" or, possibly (for the language is somewhat indefinite) of "the saints" into the hand of this Ecclesiastical despotism.

It appears then, that Ecclesiastical writers mention, as a remarkable era in the history of the Papacy, the grant, by the Imperial power, of a general or universal jurisdiction over all things pertaining to religion to the Pope of Rome, a few centuries after the establishment of Christianity under Constantine. Some difficulty however has been felt by prophetical writers in consequence of two distinct grants of this nature being recorded—the one by Justinian in the year 533, the other by Phocas, in the year 606. It will be very desirable, however, briefly, to place the facts of the case before the reader, in order that he may judge for himself in a matter of so much interest and importance.

The Emperor Justinian ascended the throne in the year 524. In the course of his spiritual legislation he issued a decree (534), in which occur the following expressions :— "We have been diligent both in *subjecting and uniting unto your holiness* (the Pope) *all the clergy* of the entire region of the East, ... and it is our firm resolve never to permit any matter touching the general state of the church to be stirred . . . . without notifying the same to your holiness, *who are the head of all the holy churches.*"—In a previous decree too he speaks of the Pope

as—"the head of all the most holy priests of God." Such
language as this naturally encouraged the Bishop of Rome to
hold himself up to the world as "the acknowledged spiritual
chief of the visible church, in every respect of rank, dignity,
and authority." And in fact this was the light in which
Pope John II. regarded these declarations; for in acknow-
ledging the edict of 534 (above quoted) he says :—
"preserving the reverence due to the Roman See, you *have
subjected all things unto her*, and reduced all churches to
that *unity which dwelleth in her alone*, to whom the Lord,
through the Prince of the Apostles, did *delegate all power.*
. . . . and that the Apostolic See is indeed *the head of all
churches*, both the rules of the fathers, and the statutes of
the princes do manifestly declare." . . . . [Greenwood's
"Cathedra Petri," ii., 134.]

Such was the first grant of universal power to the Papacy;
we now proceed to relate the second and more important
donation.

Towards the close of the sixth century, the Papal seat
was filled by Gregory the Great, whose Pontificate constituted quite an era in the history of the Papacy. This
Pontiff belonged to a class whose character must command
respect, but whose influence is at the same time the most
mischievous when exerted in the cause of error. He was
probably sincere in all he did for the advancement of
Popery, yet to him, more, perhaps than any one individual,
was the establishment of that system owing, which for
more than twelve centuries has pressed like an incubus
upon Europe. To extend the boundaries of Christendom—
to uphold the supremacy of St. Peter's chair—to connect
all the separate fountains of ecclesiastical administration

with the Papal throne, so as to bring the whole Ecclesiastical body into a compact unity over which the Bishop of Rome should preside as universal bishop, these were the objects to which he devoted all the time, and thought, and effort which he could secure from political anxieties and social calamities which agitated his mind.

It was in Gregory's reign that the jealousy which had long subsisted between the two rival Patriarchs of Rome and Constantinople broke out into a flame. The Emperor Maurice, in 588, conferred the title of Universal Patriarch upon John the Faster, Archbishop of Constantinople. Pope Pelagius at once opposed that pretension, and eight years afterwards the contest was much more vigorously renewed by Gregory. He addressed five epistles on this subject to John himself, to the Emperor and Empress, and to the rival patriarchs of Alexandria and Antioch, in all vehemently inveighing against the arrogance of the Eastern Pope, and professing the most abject humility. "Lay aside," says he, "the haughty and damnable distinction," *i. e.*, of Universal Bishop. "What reply will you make to Christ, *the only head of the Universal Church*, at the last day, for thus usurping His office?"

This renunciation, on his own behalf, of the title of Universal Bishop, shows, at least, that up to his time, the Papacy had not formally and fully established its seat at the Vatican. Still, it is well observed by an Ecclesiastical historian, that, in thus acting, "Gregory did not abandon one single article of prerogative, claimable under that title. He debarred the Bishops from the free exercise of their private judgment. He affirmed, as a matter of *legal notoriety*, that all synods or councils unsanctioned by Rome, were null and void ; and intimated that although the use of the title in question might not be *expedient*, yet, as a matter of *strict right*, the Roman Pontiff was entitled to adopt it."

Gregory was succeeded by Sabinian, but the new Pontiff held the see only five months. His successor was Boniface III, and instead of imitating the example of Gregory, in repudiating the title of Universal Bishop, he actually sought it from the hands of the civil power. His request was granted—and a decree was issued by the Emperor Phocas ordaining "the Apostolic See of Rome to be the head of all churches." Platina, a papal biographer of the fifteenth century—probably deriving his information from the Vatican Library—adds, that upon the arrival of this decree, Boniface hastened to assemble a synod, consisting of sixty-two Italian prelates, and that in conformity with, its tenor he solemnly proclaimed the holy see to be the "head of all churches," and the Pope "Universal Bishop." [Greenwood ii. p. 241.]

It is worthy of notice, too, that writers on Ecclesiastical History speak of this identical period as that in which the Papal system attained that form in which it afterwards subsisted.* The principles which gave to Romanism a lasting and definite form, and which had long been

---

* One of the ablest and most thorough works on the history of the Papacy is a work now in course of publication, entitled "Cathedra Petri, a Political History of the Great Latin Patriarchate," by THOMAS GREENWOOD, M.A. In the second volume of this masterly work, the author thus writes :—" Every principle of an unlimited religious autocracy had been avowed and adopted (during the sixth century) by or on behalf of the Holy See ; and these principles had been to a considerable extent practically established. The outward machinery of this spiritual absolutism had been put in motion, yet many impediments to the smooth working of the system still existed. But the commencement of the seventh century marks a new period in the History of the Latin Patriarchate" (p. 244).

collecting strength, were developed under the splendid Pontificate of Gregory the Great. Yet, strange to say, the Pontiff who claimed and exercised all the exorbitant powers involved in the title of Universal Bishop and head of the Church, repudiated the title. Under the reign of Boniface, this title, the only thing wanting to complete the full assumption of spiritual supremacy, was granted to that Pontiff by Imperial manifesto. And then, as we believe, and the "times and laws," and probably the saints of God—were " given into his hand," and the great period of " twelve hundred and sixty years," took their commencement.

We think then, there is the strongest ground for believing that the year 1866 or 1867 will prove, as Dr. CUMMING states, a great prophetical era—inasmuch as it clearly appears to be the end of the "time, times, and a half time." If this be true—for we would not express ourselves dogmatically on such a point—that year will be marked by some very great and decisive changes in the moral and political horizon of Europe. The great earthquake mentioned in Rev. xi. 13, will then take place—the church of God come forth from her place of refuge—all persecution for conscience sake cease—and the two witnesses of God "ascend to heaven in a cloud." But as for being, as Dr CUMMING states, the period of the coming of Christ, and the commencement of millennial blessedness, there is not the slightest evidence of anything like this, and the language of Scripture is altogether opposed to such a notion. " Of that day and of that hour knoweth no man, no not the angels in heaven, but my Father only."

CHAPTER V.

"The Great Tribulation," as described in Scripture.

"THE GREAT TRIBULATION" is the title under which Dr. CUMMING's new work on Prophecy has just been ushered into the world. We venture to say, however, that if the author had carefully studied the accounts given of that period of trouble in the Scriptures of truth, he would never have published the book. The very idea of this terrible visitation being *future* is altogether fatal to his theory of the near approach of the coming of Christ. It will be the object of the following pages to make this evident to the reader's apprehension.

"THE GREAT TRIBULATION," as it is called (Matt. xxiv. 21), denotes a period of trouble and distress, yet future, the intensity of which is such as to render it altogether *unparalleled*—In the language of Scripture, it will be such as never was, and never will be (Matt xxiv. 21). There are altogether four passages of Scripture which speak of this visitation as altogether *unparalleled*. The *first* occurs in Jeremiah xxx. 6—7 : " Ask ye now, and see whether a man doth travail with child ? wherefore do I see every man with his hands on his loins, as a woman in travail, and all faces are turned into paleness ?   Alas ! for that day is great, so THAT NONE IS LIKE IT ; it is even the time of Jacob's trouble ; but he shall be saved out of it."

The *second* occurs Dan xii. 7 :—" And there shall be a time of trouble, SUCH AS NEVER WAS since there was a nation *even* to that same time : and at that time thy people shall be delivered, every one *that shall be* found written in the book."

The *third* is found in Joel ii. 2 :—" A day of darkness and of gloominess, a day of clouds and of thick darkness, as the morning spread upon the mountains ; a great people and a strong : THERE HATH NOT BEEN EVER THE LIKE, NEITHER SHALL BE ANY MORE AFTER IT, even to the years of many generations."

The *last* passage is in Matt. xxiv. 21 :—" For then shall be great tribulation, SUCH AS WAS NOT since the beginning of the world to this time, NO, NOR EVER SHALL BE."

Now as these passages all agree in representing this period of trouble as altogether *unparalleled* in its character, there can be no doubt that they refer to the same visita-tion, since, in the very nature of things, the fact of a tribulation being such as never was and never will be again, can only apply to *one and the same event.*

Let us now ask Dr. CUMMING what are his views respecting this period of trouble ?   Strange to say, the only specific mention of the " Great Tribulation " which he has given occurs in the Preface to the work.   This the reader will probably agree with us is somewhat remarkable— considering that it professes to be the subject of the book.

The following are Dr. CUMMING's remarks on this important topic :—

"No ordinary events are looming up from every point of the European horizon, like strange birds of evil omen. All the ten years that have passed away, and the seven that still remain of the 'Great Tribulation,' will cover a time of trouble unprecedented, since there was a nation. It is the time when there 'shall be great distress of nations, with perplexity,' political, social, commercial, and moral—the disintegration of political party, the distrust of trade, the dereliction of moral obligations, confusion of principles, and collision of passions; 'the sea and the waves roaring.' There shall also be fulfilled and felt what is written in Luke :—'Men's hearts failing for fear, and for looking after those things which are coming on the earth, for the powers of heaven shall be shaken'" (pp. viii, ix).

Now, if the reader will examine for himself the inspired Prophecies from which the quotations in the previous page are taken, we think he will allow that Dr. CUMMING is altogether mistaken in his view of the "Great Tribulation." He will find the most unquestionable evidence that —(1.) This period of unparalleled trouble, instead of describing as Dr. CUMMING represents, a period of general suffering coming upon the Christian church and the world at large, denotes a judgment upon THE JEWISH NATION —(2.) Instead of "ten years" of this Great Tribulation, having "passed away" and "seven" more years "still remaining," the event is altogether FUTURE—(3.) Instead of consisting in "perplexity, political, social, commercial and moral—the disintegration of political party, the dereliction of moral obligations," &c., &c., it will evidently arise from a tremendous ATTACK UPON THE JEWISH NATION— after their restoration to the land of their fathers, by a countless host of invaders.

· *First.*—We say nothing can be clearer than the fact that
the "Great Tribulation" is confined to the *Jewish nation,*
and has, in its proper meaning, no reference to either the
Christian Church or the world at large. In the first passage
above quoted, from Jeremiah xxx. 6, the prophecy is thus
introduced.—"These are the words concerning Judah and
Israel"—and the Tribulation is termed—"Jacob's trouble,"
without any reference to the world as concerned in it. In
the *Second* passage, from Daniel, it is clearly the Jews that
are concerned. Daniel in the same verse from which the
passage is taken says, "At that time shall Michael stand
up, the great prince which standeth for the *children of thy
people*"—and the result of it is said to be :—" At that time
thy people shall be delivered ;" so that it is clearly the Jews
who are the subject of the prophecy. The *Third* passage,
beyond all doubt, is from a prophecy which from first to
last concerns the same people. The priests of the people
are urged to "stand between the porch and the altar," and
intercede with God on their behalf.—(Joel ii. 17) ; and the
language they are to use is,—"Spare Thy people, O Lord,
and give not thy heritage to reproach ; wherefore should
the heathen say—where is now your God ?" This clearly
proves that the world is exempt from this particular
trouble ; for, otherwise, if it comprehended mankind in
general, how could the Jews become "a reproach to
the heathen," as the consequence of experiencing this
visitation ? Lastly, in Matthew xxiv. 21, it must denote
some unprecedented trouble coming upon the Jewish
nation, because they are directed to flee from Jerusalem,
and also to pray that their flight "be not on the Sabbath-
day."

Secondly.—It is altogether *future*, and in the nature of things cannot occur for some years to come. The Jews must first be restored to their own land, since Judea and Jerusalem are expressly mentioned as the scene of the visitation. It may be objected by some, that the restoration of the Jews is doubtful, but there can be no question that the belief in that fact is fast gaining ground amongst those who study the word of God. It is the fashion with many expositors of Scripture in the present day, to apply the numerous predictions of this final restoration of the Jews, to the Christian church. But, in reply to this objection, we would adopt the words of the late Dr. HENDERSON, whose learned Commentaries on Isaiah, Jeremiah, and the minor Prophets, have placed Christian scholars under such lasting obligations to him. This laborious student of the Old Testament Scriptures thus expresses himself in the Preface to his Commentary and New Translation of Isaiah: —"There is (in the Old Testament Prophecies of the return of the Jews) such an obvious description of the desolation of Palestine, and such express mention of a restored land, mountains, vineyards, fields, houses, flocks, &c., which cannot be figuratively understood, that with no hermeneutical propriety can the scene be placed in the Gentile world, or regarded as exhibiting the state of Gentile Christianity."

Thirdly.—It will arise from a tremendous attack upon the city of Jerusalem, by a countless and implacable host of enemies. This is plain, if we consider the context of the passage in Joel in particular :—"A nation is come up upon my land, strong and without number, whose teeth are the teeth of a lion, and he hath the cheek teeth of a great

lion" (Joel i. 6). "Blow ye the trumpet in Zion, and sound
an alarm in my holy mountain: let all the inhabitants of the
land tremble : for the day of the Lord cometh, for it is nigh
at hand; A day of darkness and of gloominess, a day of
clouds and of thick darkness, as the morning spread upon
the mountains : a great people and a strong; there hath not
been ever the like, neither shall be any more after it, even
to the years of many generations. A fire devoureth before
them; and behind them a flame burneth : the land is as
the garden of Eden before them, and behind them a desolate
wilderness; yea, and nothing shall escape them. The
appearance of them is as the appearance of horses; and as
horsemen so shall they run. Like the noise of chariots on
the tops of mountains shall they leap, like the noise of a
flame of fire that devoureth the stubble, as a strong people
set in battle array. Before their face the people shall be
much pained: all faces shall gather blackness. They shall
run like mighty men ; they shall climb the wall like men of
war; and they shall march every one on his ways, and
they shall not break their ranks : Neither shall one thrust
another; they shall walk every one in his path : and when
they fall upon the sword, they shall not be wounded. They
shall run to and fro in the city; they shall run upon the
wall, they shall climb up upon the houses; they shall enter
in at the windows like a thief. The earth shall quake
before them; the heavens shall tremble : the sun and the
moon shall be dark, and the stars shall withdraw their
shining : And the Lord shall utter his voice before his
army : for his camp is very great : for he is strong that
executeth his word : for the day of the Lord is great and
very terrible; and who can abide it ?" (Joel ii., 1—11.)

We are aware that many Commentators explain this prophecy of Joel in a literal sense, as foretelling a plague of locusts ; but were this true, how is it that no records of such an event so altogether unprecedented have ever reached us ? We are much mistaken if the prediction has not a far more profound meaning than any plague of locusts would accomplish.

The true key to the prophecy we believe to be the following chapter, Joel iii. This chapter is connected with the second by the copulative 'for ;' and taken together they teach in the plainest manner, that the great army of locusts denotes a countless host of rapacious and irresistible enemies. They are especially described as coming from " the north" —the natural consequences are famine and all the other horrors of a siege—ending, in the first instance, in the storming and capture of the city by the foe, and ultimately in the utter destruction of the invading army, in answer to the prayers of the Jewish remnant.

The most cursory perusal of the latter portion of the prophecies of Zechariah—especially the fourteenth chapter —will convince the reader that it is the same event which is again described there :—"Behold the day of the Lord cometh, and thy spoil shall be divided in the midst of thee. For I will gather all nations against Jerusalem to battle ; and the city shall be taken, and the houses rifled, and the women ravished ; and half of the city shall go forth into captivity, and the residue of the people shall not be cut off from the city. Then shall the Lord go forth, and fight against those nations, as when he fought in the day of battle." " And men shall dwell in it, and there shall be no more utter destruction ; but Jerusalem shall be safely inhabited. And this shall be the plague wherewith the Lord will smite all the people that have fought against Jerusalem : their flesh shall consume away while they stand upon their feet, and their eyes shall consume away in their holes, and their tongue shall consume away in their mouth"—(Zechariah xiv. 1—3, and 11—13).

The same attack is evidently related by Ezekiel, in the thirty-eighth and thirty-ninth chapters of his prophecy, and many additional particulars are there given :—" And the word of the Lord came unto me, saying, Son of man, set thy face against Gog, the land of Magog, the chief prince* of Meshech and Tubal, and prophesy against him, And say, Thus saith the Lord God, behold I am against thee, O Gog, the chief prince of Meshech and Tubal ; And I will turn thee back, and put hooks into thy jaws, and I will bring thee forth, and all thine army, horses and horsemen, all of them clothed with all sorts of armour, even a great company with bucklers and shields, all of them handling swords : Persia, Ethiopia, Libya, with them ; all of them with shield and helmet : Gomer, and all his bands ; the house of Togarmah of the north quarters, and all his bands ; and many people with thee. Be thou prepared, and prepare for thyself, thou, and all thy company that are assembled unto thee, and be thou a guard unto them. After many days thou shalt be visited : in the latter years thou shalt come into the land that is brought back from the sword, and is gathered out of

* The Hebrew word here translated "chief" is רֹאשׁ (ROSH), and unquestionably means Russia. The learned Gesenius, in his Thesaurus of the Hebrew language thus translates the passage :—"Gog, prince of the land of Magog, of the Russians, the Moschi, and Tibareni." Hence, it is plain that Russia will be the leader in this enterprise. The same fact may be gathered from Dan. xi. 41, where, at the time of the end, "the king of the north enters into the glorious land," &c.

many people, against the mountains of Israel, which have
been always waste : but it is brought forth out of the
nations, and they shall dwell safely all of them. Thou
shalt ascend and come like a storm : thou shalt be like a
cloud to cover the land, thou, and all thy bands, and many
people with thee. Thus saith the Lord God, It shall also
come to pass, that at the same time shall things come into
thy mind, and thou shalt think an evil thought : And thou
shalt say, I will go up to the land of unwalled villages ; I
will go to them that are at rest, that dwell safely, all of
them dwelling without walls, and having neither bars nor
gates, To take a spoil, and to take a prey ; to turn thine
hand upon the desolate places that are now inhabited, and
upon the people that are gathered out of the nations, which
have gotten cattle and goods, that dwell in the midst of
the land"—(Ezekiel xxxviii. 1—12).

In the following chapter we have the terrible overthrow
of this vast host described :—" Therefore, thou son of man,
prophesy against Gog, and say, Thus saith the Lord God,
Behold, I am against thee, O Gog, the chief prince of
Meshech and Tubal : And I will turn thee back, and leave
but the sixth part of thee, and will cause thee to come up
from the north parts, and will bring thee upon the mountains of Israel : And I will smite thy bow out of thy left
hand, and will cause thine arrows to fall out of thy right
hand. Thou shalt fall upon the mountains of Israel, thou,
and all thy bands, and the people that is with thee : I will
give thee unto the ravenous birds of every sort, and to the
beasts of the field to be devoured. Thou shalt fall upon
the open field ; for I have spoken it, saith the Lord God.
And I will send a fire on Magog, and among them that

dwell carelessly in the isles ; and they shall know that I am the Lord. So will I make My holy name known in the midst of My people Israel ; and I will not let them pollute My holy name any more : and the heathen shall know that I am the Lord, the Holy One in Israel. Behold, it is come, and it is done, saith the Lord God ; this is the day whereof I have spoken. And they that dwell in the cities of Israel shall go forth, and shall set on fire and burn the weapons, both the shields and the bucklers, the bows and the arrows, and the hand-staves, and the spears, and they shall burn them with fire seven years" (Ezekiel xxxix. 1—9).

There is another Prophecy, referring to a period just *after* the Millenium, in Rev. xx. 8, which introduces Gog and Magog, a circumstance that has led many to refer this Prophecy of Ezekiel to the same period. But the attack described by Ezekiel must occur *before* the Millennium, as the slightest examination of the two chapters will prove. It is distinctly stated that the conversion of the Jews takes place as the result of, and after, the battle:— " The house of Israel shall know that I am the Lord their God from that day and forward"—(xxxix. 22) ; " So will I make My holy name known in the midst of My people Israel ; and I will not let them pollute My holy name any more"—(7). Besides, other passages plainly intimate that the issue of the battle will be instrumental in diffusing the knowledge and glory of God throughout the world ; which is a plain proof that it takes place before the Millennium. —(See xxxviii. 23, and xxxix. 7—21).

If the above be the true Scriptural account of the "Great Tribulation" of the latter days, it will be obvious that Dr.

CUMMING is altogether mistaken in his recent work on that subject. He is in error as regards the people who experience this visitation—as regards the period of its occurrence—and as regards the nature of the Tribulation.

There is another inference, also, which we are justified in drawing from the foregoing remarks. If this account of the Great Tribulation be the Scriptural one, then Dr. CUMMING's theory as to the year 1867 being the coming of the Son of man, and the end of the world, is simply IMPOSSIBLE. The Jews are not yet restored to their own land. There are no immediate signs of such an event being near. If it should commence next year, even, it must, in the very nature of things, occupy some considerable time. If to this delay we add the time consumed in organising a confederation against Jerusalem, and the period occupied in the siege of the city, it is certain that at the very least some two or three years, from the present time, must elapse before the Great Tribulation occurs. Now, as we are expressly told, that after all is over, seven years more will be occupied in burning the weapons of war belonging to the invading army (Ezek. xxxix, 9), it is certain that the coming of Christ cannot take place, as Dr. CUMMING "is satisfied" it will, in 1867, because, as he himself states, that coming will be attended with a conflagration which will consume all terrestrial things.

CHAPTER VI.

The Future of Europe.

ON the pouring out of the SEVENTH VIAL, a great voice is heard from the throne of God—proclaiming the ominous words "IT IS DONE!" As regards this terrific judgment, Dr. CUMMING gives us his views of it, in the Preface to his "Great Tribulation." He says, "I stated in 'Apocalyptic Sketches,' that the last Vial—that is the symbol which denotes the source and measure and duration of the 'Great Tribulation'—was, in all probability, poured out in 1848, from which time to 1867 we may expect to feel its intensest effects"—(p. 1). He afterwards proceeds to mention what he considers to have been the results of this Vial, up to the present time. These are the potato and vine blight—cholera and diptheria—the Continental revolutions of 1848—the Russian war—the earthquake at Naples—the commercial panic of 1857—the present universal derangement of social and national life—"and if one might enumerate the incessant murders, and suicides, and poisonings with which the papers teem, of moral life also"—the Italian war, just over—and the present unsettled state of Europe and Asia.

In opposition to this theory, we will now, with the reader's permission, endeavour to show what is the Scriptural account of this last and closing judgment of the Most High ; believing as we do that the statements of Dr. CUMMING are altogether erroneous, and that the fearful judgment of the Seventh Vial is wholly FUTURE. We begin by observing—what the attentive student of the Apocalypse has probably observed—that the grand catastrophe of this *Seventh Vial* has already been twice pourtrayed in this mysterious book.—*First,* under the *Sixth Seal,* and then again under the *Seventh Trumpet.* Indeed, each of the great *series* of visions, which the Apocalypse contains—the Seals, Trumpets, and Vials—all end in the grand finale. (See Rev. vi. 12—17. xi. 17—19 and xvi. 18—21). So that the Apocalypse resembles some work on history, for instance, in which the author goes over the same ground again in two or three successive chapters, in order to contemplate the same period from different stand-points. Thus, as we view the prophecy, the Seals sketch the successive phases of the Church, from the times of Apostolic purity ("a white horse"), down to those of Papal corruption ("a pale or livid-green horse") : and close with the long-delayed vengeance on the Apostate Church, under the Sixth Seal. The Seventh Seal introduces the Seven Trumpets, under which the *political* history of Christendom seems to be sketched during the same period of time as that embraced in the Seals. The Seventh *Trumpet*— though perhaps of wider import—describes substantially the same great event as the Sixth Seal—the final vengeance of God on the persecutors of His people. The Seven *Vials* again seem to be chiefly an expansion of this

Seventh Trumpet, the Seventh Vial being nearly identical with its close.*

It is thus evident, we think, that each of the three series of apocalyptic visions—the Seals, the Trumpets, and the Vials—ends with the same grand catastrophe—the winding up of the Divine scheme—the last act in the mighty drama which forms the subject of the book. We do not assert that the Sixth Seal, the Seventh Trumpet, and the Seventh Vial are identical, neither do we think they are precisely synchronous. But all three agree in this, that they contain the great *finale* which closes the present dispensation.

The leading event in the catastrophe of the Seventh Vial is clearly the battle of Armageddon. The mustering of the hosts is mentioned at the close of the Sixth Vial : "and he gathered them together unto a place called in the Hebrew tongue, Armageddon," (xvi. 16). But the actual conflict occurs under the next Vial, when the voice from the throne proclaims—"It is done !" This fearful conflict— a universal war, undertaken apparently to defeat the purposes of God—is described more fully in the nineteenth chapter :

---

* The Seventh Trumpet evidently contains the Seven Vials, but as it is never once mentioned throughout his work on "The Great Tribulation," possibly Dr. CUMMING may regard it as yet future, while holding that the Seven Vials are already poured out. This will not at all affect any remarks made by the writer in the previous part of the work, as there is positively nothing in the Seventh Trumpet which is not included in the Vials. If therefore an Expositor of Prophecy admits the latter to be past, it is very unimportant whether the former be so or not. But in fact, it can be easily demonstrated that if the Seven Vials are poured out, as Dr. CUMMING asserts, the Seventh Trumpet has sounded. The proof is as follows—The Vials are expressly said to be "the Seven LAST plagues," and in them "is FILLED UP the wrath of God." This being the case, since the Seventh Trumpet is the last of the three woe-trumpets, and on its sounding, the four-and-twenty elders praise God that His "wrath is come," (xi. 18), it is certain it cannot sound after the Seven Vials are poured out. To assert the contrary, is to maintain that the wrath of God can be inflicted after it "is filled up," and other plagues endured after the last plague (the Seventh Vial) has been experienced.

—" And I saw heaven opened, and behold a white horse ; and he that sat upon him was called Faithful and True ; and in righteousness he doth judge and make war. His eyes were as a flame of fire, and on his head were many crowns ; and he had a name written that no man knew but he himself : And he was clothed with a vesture dipped in blood : and his name is called The Word of God. And the armies which were in heaven followed him upon white horses, clothed in fine linen, white and clean. And out of his mouth goeth a sharp sword, that with it he should smite the nations ; and he shall rule them with a rod of iron : and he treadeth the wine-press of the fierceness and wrath of Almighty God. And he hath on his vesture and on his thigh a name written, KING OF KINGS AND LORD OF LORDS. . . . . And I saw the beast, and the kings of the earth, and their armies, gathered together to make war against him that sat on the horse, and against his army" (Rev. xix. 11—16, and 19).

A careful comparison of the inspired accounts of this terrible conflict, with the attack on the Jews described in Ezekiel, Joel, and Zechariah, will, we think, satisfy the student of Prophecy, that these events are *one* and *the same*. The limits of this little work will not allow us to enter fully into the details of this subject ; but we may mention some of the principal points of identity, for the reader's consideration.

(1.) Both will consist in a universal war, entered upon by the kings of the whole earth against "the people of God." (See Joel iii. 2 ; Ezek. xxxviii. 3, 5, 6 ; Zech. xiv. 2 ; Rev, xix. 19.)

(2.) Both contain the remarkable summons to all the

fowls of heaven to come and feast upon the carcases of
princes and nobles, and captains, &c. &c. (See Ezek.
xxxix. 17—20 ; Rev. xix. 17, 18).

(3.) The period of millennial blessedness appears to be the
immediate result of this concluding Vial of Divine wrath.
In the prophecies of Zechariah and Joel, the copious and
general outpouring of the Holy Spirit is mentioned as
taking place immediately after the conflict. In Ezekiel too,
the nine following chapters are occupied with a description
of the building of the Temple, generally considered to refer
to Millennial times ; and the chapter following the battle
of Armageddon in the Revelation, commences with the
binding of Satan, and commencement of the Millennium.

The awful catastrophe which forms the subject of this
chapter is not peculiar to the Apocalypse, nor indeed to the
New Testament. It is depicted in many parts of the prophetical writings of the Old Testament. One of the most
explicit statements is that contained in Daniel's account of
the Vision of Nebuchadnezzar. That king, we read, was
favoured with a vision of an image symbolical of the four
successive forms which the world-power would assume
down to "the time of the end." This image's "head was
of fine gold, his breast and his arms of silver, his belly
and his thighs of brass, his legs of iron, his feet part of iron
and part of clay." According to all Prophetical writers, the
feet represent the modern kingdoms of . Europe. Let
the reader mark what follows. "Thou sawest," says
the angel, "till that a stone was cut out without hands,
which smote the image upon his feet, that were of iron,
and clay, and brake them to pieces. Then was the iron
the clay, the brass, the silver, and the gold, broken to

pieces together, and became like the chaff of the summer threshing-floors ; and the wind carried them away, that no place was found for them ; and the stone that smote the image became a great mountain, and filled the whole earth." (Dan. ii. 34, 35).

The reader cannot fail to observe the identity of this terrible destruction with the catastrophe of the Sixth Seal, Seventh Trumpet, and Seventh Vial. It will be observed, the utter overthrow of the world-power is clearly described in both ; but, on comparing the two Prophecies together, we shall find progression in some points, corresponding to the relation of the New Testament and the Old. One lesson, however, is taught with as much clearness as in any part of the Apocalypse, and that is, that the kingdoms of this world must first be *destroyed*, before they can become the kingdoms of God and of Christ. "The stone," we read, *first* "smote the image, and *then* became a great mountain, and filled the whole earth."

On this point the remarks of AUBERLEN are worthy of profound attention. "Christianity exerts an ennobling influence on all spheres of life ; but a transfiguration, in the correct sense of the word, must first be preceded by a regeneration, a palingenesis. First, there must be death and resurrection, even as our Lord had to pass through this path to His transfiguration. The kingdoms of this world— that is the simple and clear meaning of our prophecy— must first be *destroyed ;* then only is it possible, that rising in a new form, they will become kingdoms of God and his Christ"* (p. 228).

* AUBERLEN on "Daniel and the Revelation." Translated from the German, and published by Messrs. Clark, Edinburgh, 1856.

It is to be regretted, that the church of God, in the present day, seems altogether ignorant of this fact, so plainly taught in the Scriptures of truth. One can hardly imagine a greater contrast than that presented by the current views on this subject and Prophecy. Christian ministers and teachers write and speak as though, ere long, the nations of Europe would be converted to God, and the whole world brought under the influence of the Gospel, by the various agencies now in operation. Such views, however, are wholly unsupported by the Word of God. Indeed, the very contrary to this is there taught. In proof of which we might allude to the striking fact that Daniel, in his prophecy of the four monarchies of the world,—both under the symbol of the *Image*, and that of the *Four Beasts—wholly overlooks the First Coming of Christ.* His *Second* Coming, (whether it be personal or figurative) is prominently dwelt upon ; but the *First* Coming is wholly unnoticed. The introduction of Christianity, and its effects upon the world down to the time of the end, find no place in his prophecy. For this remark we are indebted to AUBERLEN, who well observes :—" What strikes us as peculiar and startling in Daniel's representation of the four monarchies is, that the First Coming of Christ,—His Church, and her influence on the development of the world, are left altogether unnoticed and unmentioned. The fourth monarchy, though Christianized for a Millenium and a half, is not distinguished either from the preceding heathen monarchies as such, or from its own heathen portion ; on the contrary, it is represented as the most terrible and as the most God-opposed of all kingdoms. God thus speaks of the world-power in its Christian period, without

mentioning at all its Christianity, only its final adherence
to Antichrist is spoken of. . . . . The kingdom of God
enters his horizon at that point where it begins to be a real
and external power of the world ; that is, at the Second
Coming of Christ. But we may learn from this a very
important lesson, viz., that, even during the Christian
period of the world's history, the old character of the world
is essentially existing ; that the outward Christianity which
the kingdoms of the world have adopted, for fifteen
centuries, is very far from real Christianity ; but that the
kingdom of God is a hidden and suffering one, till the Lord
Jesus comes again. Roos remarks (p. 70),—' The Roman
empire was worldly as long as it was heathen ; it has re-
mained worldly, though it has become Christian'" (p.225).

These remarks contain profound truth. They are true,
whatever view we take of the Second Coming of Christ—
whether we view it as personal or figurative. The plain
fact cannot be denied—cannot be concealed. The present
despotisms of Europe will not quietly and peacefully give way
before the spread of the kingdom of Christ. The ecclesiastical Hierarchies of Europe will not gradually disappear before the steady march of liberty, truth, and righteousness.
No! Destruction—sudden, violent and tremendous—over-
takes them in the midst of their career. The stone *smites*
the image upon its feet, and *breaks them to pieces !* But this
fact, instead of discouraging the servants of Christ, should
lead them to redouble their energies in missionary work
and home operations. We should "work while it is called
to-day, for the night cometh when no man can work."

It is probably with reference to the tremendous overthrow described in these predictions, that Daniel mentions

a further period of twelve hundred and ninety days (xii, 2). Dr. CUMMING, as we have seen in the passage extracted from him, (page 8 of this work) adds the additional thirty days, or years, to the year 1792, thus arriving at 1822. But of what conceivable event was that the era? Let any reader search the chronological tables of Europe, and tell us what event worthy of the slightest notice took place then. This, of itself is sufficient to prove the fallacy of Dr. CUMMING's calculations. For, the "twelve hundred and ninety years" must mark a great, and most momentous era. Unless Dr. CUMMING can find some great, and marked, and clearly defined event in 1822, all his calculations must fall to the ground. We challenge him to the proof. We would be very cautious in expressing any positive opinion on the subject of dates, but, there does seem some ground to believe that the thirty additional years refers to the battle of Armageddon—the final overthrow of the combined forces of the beast and the false prophet—Civil and Ecclesiastical Despotism. This might naturally be expected about *thirty* years after the year 1866—the end of the time, times, and half a time. In this case, the further period of *forty-five* years (Dan. xii. 12) probably refers to the full establishment of the kingdom of God on earth—this being the only period with which a blessing is associated. "Blessed is he that waiteth and cometh to the thousand three hundred and five and thirty days."

W. MACK, PRINTER, WINE STREET, BRISTOL.